The Little Bully

witten by Adam and Charlotte Guillain

illustrated by Jennifer A. Bell

Billy was a great boy. He was always friendly and kind and had a **big** smile for everyone.

Raintree is an imprint of Capstone Global Library Limited,
a company incorporated in England and Wales having its
registered office at 7 Pilgrim Street, London, EC4V 6LB –
Registered company number: 6695582

To contact Raintree:
Phone: 0845 6044371
Fax: + 44 (0) 1865 312263
Email: myorders@raintreepublishers.co.uk
Outside the UK please telephone +44 1865 312262.

First published by © Picture Window Books in 2011
First published in the United Kingdom in paperback in 2014
The moral rights of the proprietor have been asserted.

Designer: Kay Fraser
Editor: Catherine Veitch
Originated by Capstone Global Library Ltd
Printed and bound in China

ISBN 978 1 4062 6621 4 (paperback)
18 17 16 15 14 13
10 9 8 7 6 5 4 3 2 1

British Library Cataloguing in Publication Data
A full catalogue record for this book is available from
the British Library.

Billy had **lots** of friends and nobody was
ever mean to him...

... apart from **Jake**.

Jake was always picking on Billy.

When Billy spilled food on his T-shirt, Jake pointed and **laughed**.

"**Ha ha**, Billy's a baby!"

If Billy made mistakes when he was writing,
Jake would say,

"Ha ha, Billy can't write his own name!"

One day Billy brought a picture he had painted of his family to school. He was really pleased with it.

But Jake just laughed when he saw it.
"**Ha ha**, Billy used pink paint. Pink is for **girls**!" Jake shouted.

Billy wanted to stand up to Jake. But whatever he said,
Jake just **laughed** even more.

It made Billy feel **horrible**.

Billy started to think
he wasn't very **clever**.

Or **funny**.

Or **nice** to look at.

Billy started to think that **everybody** was laughing at him.

Billy didn't want to go to school any more. But he didn't tell his mum and dad the reason why.

Instead Billy said, "School is **stupid**. I want to stay at home."

"But school is **fun**!" Dad told him.

"And you're doing really well!" said Mum.

So Billy had to go to school and Jake kept teasing him.

One day, Billy wore a new T-shirt to school.

Jake laughed when he saw Billy.

"Ha ha, you're wearing **baby** clothes!" Jake shouted.

Billy knew his T-shirt wasn't for babies. His baby sister didn't wear T-shirts like his. Why was Jake being so **mean**?

Billy thought about it. Then he realised that Jake didn't have any other friends apart from him. It would be **easy** to pick on Jake.

Billy looked at Jake. His T-shirt had a bear

on it. He'd spilled paint on his clothes.

And his shoelaces were undone.

But Billy didn't want to pick on Jake. He knew how **hard** it was to tie shoelaces.

And he **liked** Jake's bear T-shirt.

And **everyone** had spilled paint on their clothes that morning.

So Billy tried something new.

"I **like** this T-shirt," he said bravely. "It's **not** for babies."

"Well, your trousers are covered in paint!"
Jake **shouted.**

"So are yours!" said Billy. "Please **stop** being so mean or I won't play with you any more."

Billy knew Jake had no-one else to play with.

Jake knew it, too.

After that, Jake stopped picking on Billy. In fact, he stopped being mean to everyone and soon he had **lots** of friends.

Just like **Billy**.